Who's That Banging on the Ceiling?

Colin McNaughton

WALKER BOOKS
AND SUBSIDIARIES
LONDON • BOSTON • SYDNEY

For Françoise, Ben and Tim

First published 1992 by Walker Books Ltd
87 Vauxhall Walk, London SE11 5HJ

This edition published 1994

Reprinted 1995, 1999

Printed in Hong Kong/China

British Library Cataloguing in Publication Data
A catalogue record for this book is
available from the British Library.

ISBN 0-7445-3165-9

Home Sweet Home!

"What's that clack, clack, clacking
on the ceiling?" says Mrs Manky
on the ground floor...

"It sounds like a dinosaur dancing the fandango!"

But that would be silly!
"What's that boing, boing, boinging?"
says Mrs Fettle on the first floor...

"It sounds like elephants on pogo sticks!"

But that would be silly!

"What's that splish, splosh, splashing?"

says Mrs Dutz on the second floor…

"It sounds like a sea battle!"

But that would be silly!
"What's that grunt, snort, slobbering?"
says Mrs Gowk on the third floor...

"It sounds like a pigsty!"

But that would be silly!
"What's that squeak, squeak, squeaking?"
says Mr Clarts on the fourth floor...

"It sounds like giant mice!"

But that would be silly!
"What's that crash, boom, twanging?"
says Mrs Tarly-Toot on the fifth floor...

"It sounds like a rock and roll show!"

But that would be silly!
"What's that moo, cluck, quacking?"
says Mr Plodge on the sixth floor...

"It sounds like a farmyard!"

But that would be silly!
"What's that ow, ouch, yowing?"
says Mrs Haddaway on the seventh floor...

"It sounds like a fight!"

But that would be silly!
"What's that argh-ee-argh-ee-arghing?"
says Mr Chebble on the eighth floor...

"It sounds like Tarzan of the Apes!"

But that would be silly!
"What's that huff, puff, puffing?"
says Mrs Gadgee on the ninth floor...

"It sounds like the big bad wolf!"

But that would be silly!
"What's that zap, bleep, blooping?"
says Mr Dunch on the tenth floor...

"It sounds like an alien invasion!"

Caw!

Bang!
Bang! Bang!
Bang!

Now that really *would* be silly!

But that would be silly!
"Who's that banging on the ceiling?"
says Mrs Hacky-Mucky on the top floor...

“It sounds
like King Kong
tap-dancing!”

This monkey is nuts!

The End!